AB Gets His Wings

Richard Bland

Published in 2019 by SilverWood Books

SilverWood Books Ltd
14 Small Street, Bristol, BS1 1DE, United Kingdom
www.silverwoodbooks.co.uk

ISBN 978-1-78132-553-7

British Library Cataloguing in Publication Data
A CIP catalogue record for this book is available
from the British Library

Page design and typesetting by SilverWood Books
Printed on responsibly sourced paper

Thank you to all who have helped with this book,
in particular Peter Collins.
'Blue Skies Red 4'

GAME
DOG

AB had been on the shelf for far too long. Every day he sat high up on the warehouse racks and watched as the machines picked out other toys and dropped them into baskets. He thought about the lucky boy or girl who would be getting them for a birthday or Christmas present. *When was it going to be his turn?*

Today had been a very long day. He was looking forward to night-time when he could climb down and meet his friends. He loved to spend time with the planes. They would give him a ride around the warehouse, flying past the other toys and making them jump!

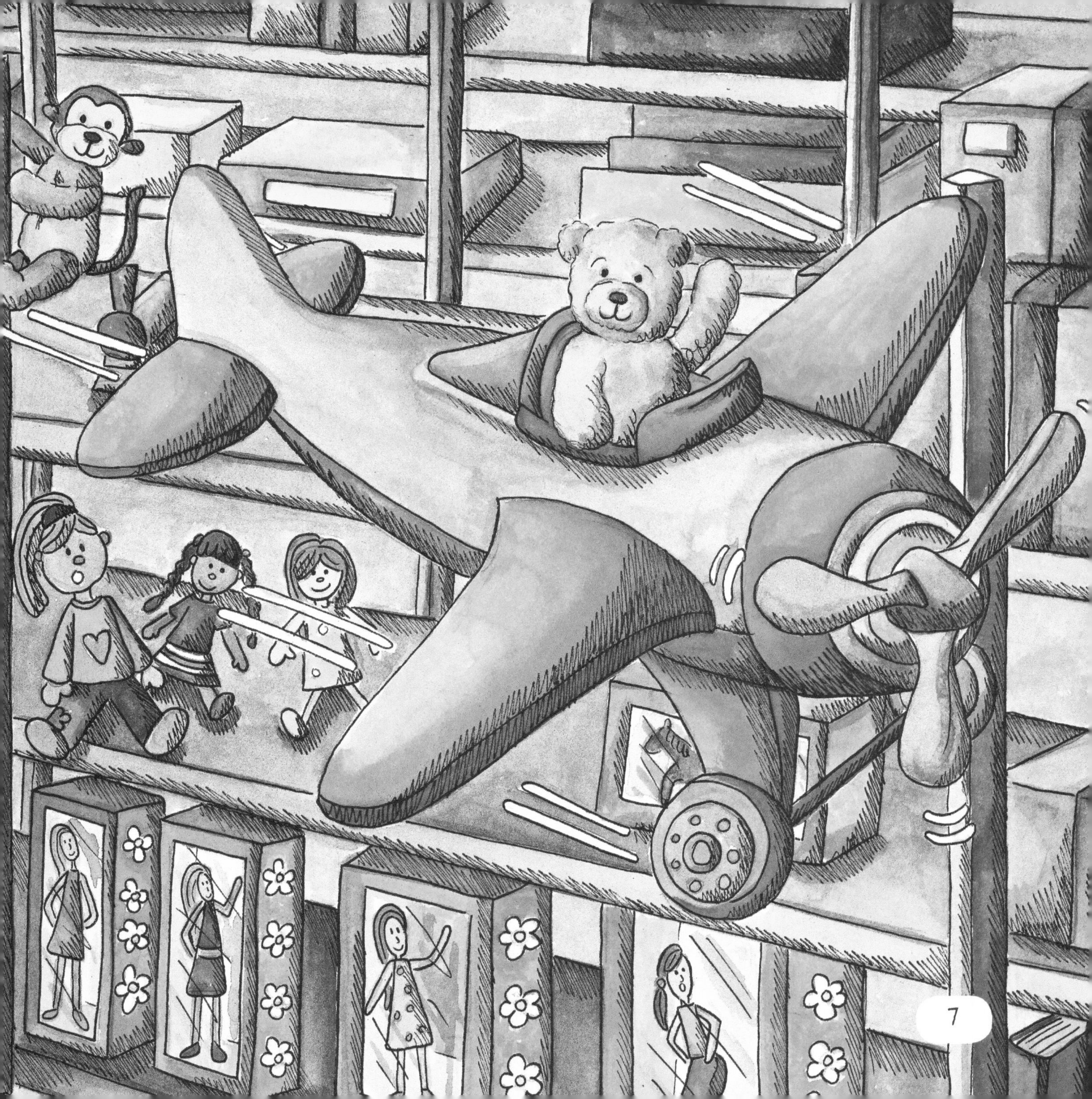

Suddenly, he was startled by a beeping sound from one of the pickers. Closer and closer it came. The long metal arm of the machine reached out to grab him. "Ouch!" he squealed, as he was grabbed by the leg, tipped upside down and dropped into a metal basket!

AB was suddenly afraid. *Where was he going? Who had picked him out? Would his new owner be a nice, kind child? Would they play with him, or just leave him in a cupboard?* Maybe, if he was really lucky, he might be someone's extra special toy, being cuddled and kept warm at night. Well, he'd just have to wait and see!

AB waved to the other toys, who were seeing him off. As he passed the planes, he gave them a 'thumbs up' to let them know he was okay. He'd miss them of course, but he was ready now for his big adventure into the wide, wide world.

The metal basket tipped him out into a cardboard box with a uniform and hat inside. ‘Oh,’ he thought, ‘maybe I’ll get to wear that.’ He tried to peer over the top, and could just see the label. The island of Anglesey was where he was headed.

Teddy
Gear

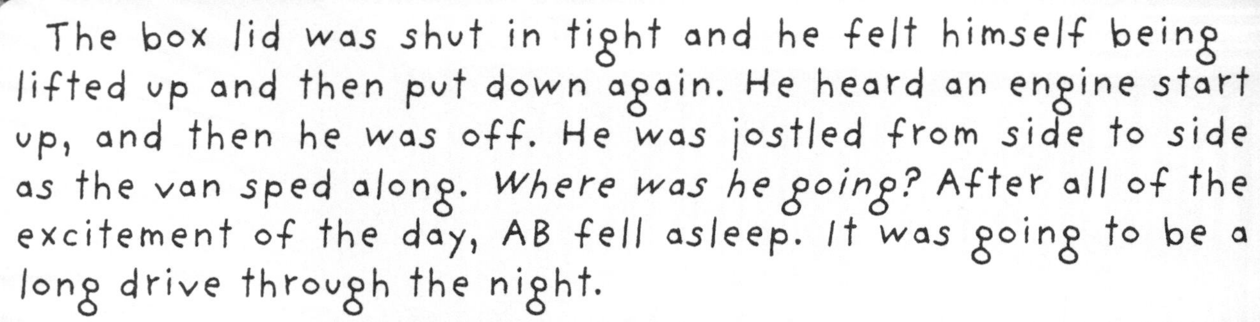

The box lid was shut in tight and he felt himself being lifted up and then put down again. He heard an engine start up, and then he was off. He was jostled from side to side as the van sped along. *Where was he going?* After all of the excitement of the day, AB fell asleep. It was going to be a long drive through the night.

Teddy Gear

Suddenly, he was woken by a jolt. Everything was quiet. He'd arrived. AB felt the box being lifted up again. He heard a door open. A man said, "Parcel for Station Commander, Group Captain Hill".
"Thanks," said another voice. "Just place it there."

AB sat very still. There was a tearing sound as the box was opened, and AB found himself staring into the eyes of a pilot! 'Gosh,' he thought. 'Where am I?' As if to answer him, Group Captain Hill exclaimed, "Welcome to your new home. Let's see how these fit on you."

AB was lifted out of the box, and felt himself being squeezed into his new outfit – it was an RAF flying suit and a blue hat to match! He caught a glimpse of his reflection through the window. ‘Cool!’ he thought. ‘This looks like it’s going to be fun.’

ROYAL AIR FORCE
QJOK

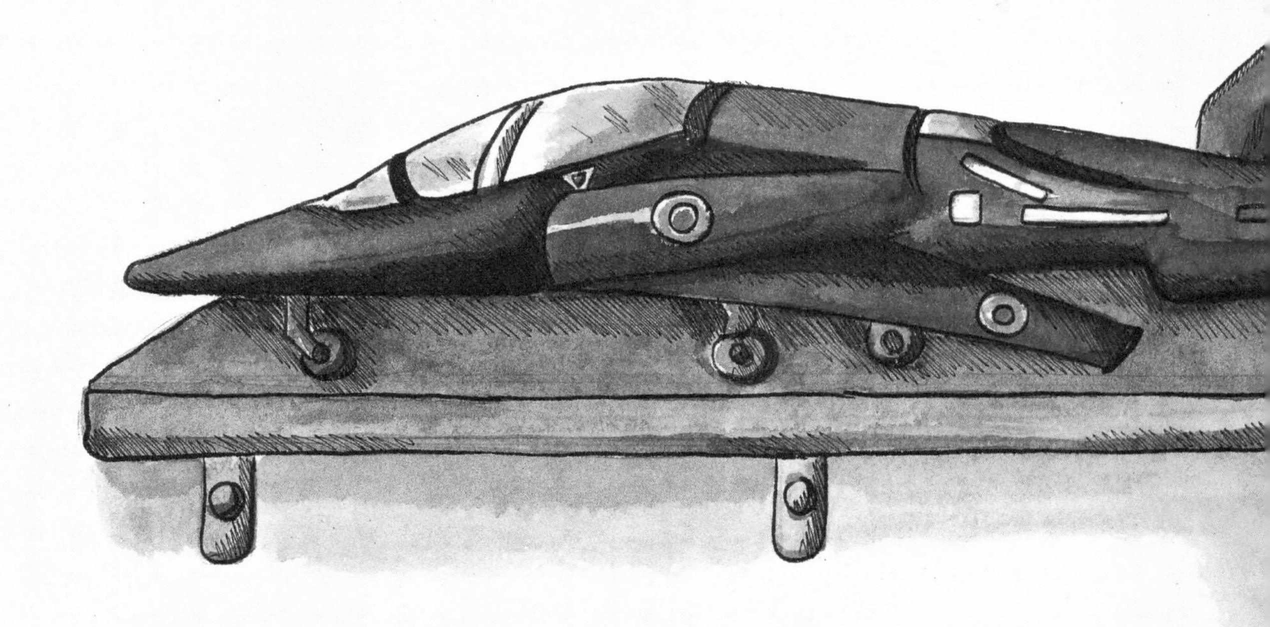

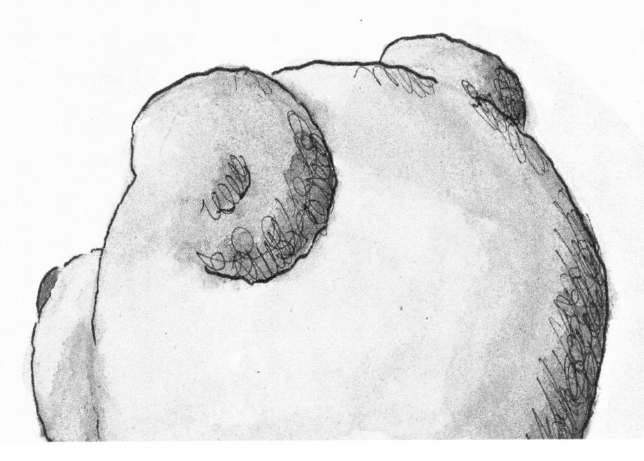

He looked around the room, and to his amazement, saw that it was full of miniature planes. 'Hurray! This is going to be like being back in the warehouse!' He smiled to himself.

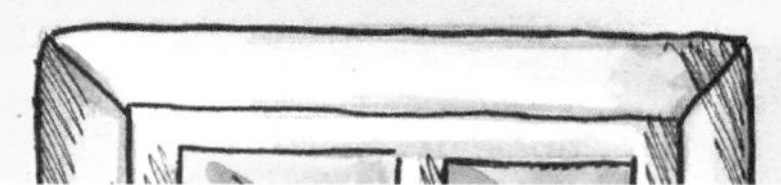

Group Captain Hill picked him up and carried him into the room next door, where a lady was waiting for him.

"Hi Molly, our new mascot has arrived. Say hello to AB. He's here for his medical before he's allowed to go up."

"Okay," replied Molly. "Let's have a look at you, then."

AB sat on the desk and was prodded and poked until he felt all the stuffing was going to come out of him! He heard the machines beeping and was put on the scales to be weighed. He was very relieved when Molly said, “Yes, he’s passed the test. He’s fighting fit and ready for action!”

'Wow, ready for action,' thought AB. 'What does that mean?'
Group Captain Hill carried him out into the yard.
"Meet your new Mascot," he said to a group of pilots and engineers that had gathered. "This is AB – he's just passed his medical and is going up for his maiden flight this afternoon!"

AB couldn't believe his ears. No longer was he just going to sit in toy planes and fly around a warehouse at night – he was going to fly in a *real* plane with *real* pilots!
"Okay, who's taking him out? Ricko, Fritzy, Puppy?"

"I will, Sir," said Flight Lieutenant Ricko. "He can come out for a quick spin in my Hawk this afternoon. I'll take him to look at the beautiful Welsh countryside."
'Gosh,' thought AB, 'this doesn't seem real. Only yesterday, I was stuck on a warehouse shelf with only toy planes to play with, and wondering if I'd ever to get to see the outside world. Here I am today, about to go up in a real life plane. I must be dreaming!'

AB was taken into the flight training room, and was put in a chair among the other pilots. He looked around to see that there were eight pilots in the room. They were being given their instructions for the training session. It all looked very complicated. They had maps on their desks and lots of technical equipment surrounded the room. The pilots were given their instructions, gathered their papers and went to their locker rooms to get kitted out. “Looks like you’re ready to go, AB!” said Ricko. “Nice outfit, but you’re missing something off your hat. Still, we’ll get that sorted, once you’ve done your first flight!”

Once all the pilots had changed into their outfits, they went outside to the hangar, where the planes were lined up. A group of engineers were checking them over. "All sorted, Sir," said Jimbo, who had given them the final nod. "Ready for take-off."

"Thanks, good to go, guys," said Ricko. "Meet AB, our newest arrival – he's off for a training flight this afternoon."
Ricko climbed into the cockpit, followed by his Number Two, and placed AB beside the controls.
"Let's get your belt on and if you feel unwell, don't forget to put on your oxygen mask," he told AB.

Suddenly, AB heard a big roar and felt a huge shudder go through the plane as it moved forward towards the runway. Faster and faster it went. Soon he was in the air, racing towards the big blue sky. 'Amazing!' he thought.

AB whooshed through the clouds, swerving past mountains, racing low over the fields. They soared higher and higher as the planes turned and twisted, circled around each other, and passed in quick formation. They finished with a loop-the-loop as they came in past the control tower to land.

"WHOA!" shouted AB. "That was the best day ever!"
"It's not finished yet," said Flt Lt Ricko. "Look what we've got for you." He showed AB a little blue box, and opened it up. It was a small shiny badge.

Ricko took it out of the box and pinned it onto AB's beret. "Well, if you're going to be the Station Mascot, you've got to look the part of an RAF pilot," he said. AB smiled to himself. 'What a day,' he thought. Little did he know that this was only the start of his adventures...

Lightning Source UK Ltd.
Milton Keynes UK
UKHW050618111219
355150UK00002B/49/P